Take a Bow, BABIES!

Based on the TV series *Rugrats*® created by Arlene Klasky, Gabor Csupo, and Paul Germain as seen on Nickelodeon®

SIMON SPOTLIGHT
An imprint of Simon & Schuster Children's Publishing Division
1230 Avenue of the Americas, New York, New York 10020

Printed in Mexico
First Edition
2 4 6 8 10 9 7 5 3 1

Gold, Rebecca.
Take a bow, babies! / by Becky Gold ; illustrated by Studio Orlando. 1st ed.
p. cm. — (Ready-to-read. Level 2)
Based on the TV series Rugrats.
Summary: Angelica and the babies find a way to participate in the library talent
show fundraiser.
ISBN 0-689-82830-6 (pbk.)
[1. Talent shows Fiction. 2. Babies Fiction.] I. Studio Orlando, ill. II. Rugrats
(Television program). III. Title. IV. Series.
PZ7.G5634Tak 2000
[E]—dc21
99-31387
CIP

Take a Bow, BABIES!

by Becky Gold
illustrated by Studio Orlando

Ready-to-Read

Simon Spotlight/Nickelodeon

New York   London   Toronto   Sydney   Singapore

4

It was a busy morning. Tommy was playing with his brother, Dil. His mom, Didi, was making pom-poms.

"I have to get these done for the talent show at the library," Didi told Grandma Minka. "I hope lots of people come."

"And I hope my matzo balls win us the trip to Sugarland Park Hotel," said Minka.

Later, Chuckie, Phil, and Lil came over.
"Guess what, guys," said Tommy.
"The liberry is having a tell-and-show!"
"What's a tell-and-show?" asked Phil.
Tommy thought for a minute. "Well, you gots to tell and show people you can do something real good," he said. "Like jump real high!"

Just then Angelica came in. "My daddy told me all about this talent show," she said. "And I'm gonna win that trip to Sugarland Park! It must be filled with cookies and candies and chocolates—"

"Baa, baa!" said Dil.

Angelica frowned. "You sound like a sheep," she said.

"How are you gonna win, Angelica?" asked Tommy.

"I'm thinking, I'm thinking," she said. Angelica watched Tommy jump.

"Baa, baa," Dil said again.

"Hmm," said Angelica. "Jumping sheep . . ."

"I got it!" Angelica yelled. "I'll be Little Go Peek, and you can be my little losted sheep!"

"What do you mean?" asked Phil.

"All you babies have to do is jump around and say 'baa,'" Angelica said. "I'll herb you together."

"Do we gots to?" Chuckie moaned.

"You do if you want to go to Sugarland Park!" she said. "Now, jump! Baa!"

The babies baaed
and jumped until it
was time for juice
and cookies.

"What's your grandma gonna do with those lotsa balls?" Chuckie asked Tommy.

"She's takin' them to the tell-and-show," Tommy said.

"Are they gonna get losted too?" asked Lil.

"No, people just gots to eat them," Tommy explained.

Angelica asked, "Aunt Didi, may I please have some pom-poms?"

"Why, yes, Angelica," replied Didi.

"Hey, what's that funny sound?"
Chuckie asked.

The babies toddled into the living
room.

"Hey, sprouts!" said Grandpa Lou.
"Listen to my talent show act. Here's my
white-breasted nuthatch." He whistled
a tune. "And this is my yellow finch." He
whistled another tune.

"Those are funny names for songs,"
Lil whispered to Phil.

Soon Angelica's dad, Drew, came to pick her up.

"Oh, Drew," said Didi, "let's see how your talent show act is coming along."

Drew took out some juggling balls and began to juggle them.

"That's great!" said Didi.

Finally, it was time for the talent show.
The grown-ups were ready with their acts.
They didn't know the babies had one too!

"Okay, babies," Angelica whispered.
"Hold still while I glue on your tails.
'Member what you're s'posed to do!"

Sugarland Park, here I come! she
thought.

19

When everyone was ready, the show started. A man walked onto the stage.

"Welcome to our talent show!" he said. "I'm your emcee, Pete Sakes. And now, hot from the pot, are Minka's light and fluffy matzo balls!"

"Come up and try some!" Minka cried.

"And now," said Pete, "here's Drew 'Butterfingers' Pickles!"

The lights on the stage were bright—too bright. Instead of his juggling balls, Drew picked up some matzo balls.

"Ouch, hot!" he cried. *Splish! Splat!* The matzo balls fell onto the stage.

Everyone laughed! They thought it was all part of Drew's act.

24

Pete came back onto the stage. "A big hand for 'Butterfingers' Pickles, everyone!" he called out. "And now, here's Lou 'the Hawk' Pickles and his birdcalls!"

Grandpa Lou's birdcalls were so good that birds started flying into the library!

They flew to the stage and pecked at the mushed matzo balls.

"Okay, babies," said Angelica. "I'm goin' out there while the goin' is good. Stay here until I wave to you."

Angelica skipped onto the stage. "I will sing a special song!" she cried.

"Little Go Peek had lotsa sheep,
But they were always losted.
So ever-where that Go Peek went,
She won first prize in the show!"

Then she danced around the stage and waved to the audience.

"Hey look, guys," Tommy said. "Angelica's waving. Let's go!"

"Jump!" shouted Phil.

"Wag your trails!" Lil added.

The babies toddled out. Angelica tried to stop them, but the babies jumped and baaed and wagged their tails.

Angelica was mad. She had not waved to the babies! And the audience loved the act!

"Well," Pete said, "they weren't on the list, but the winners are Little Go Peek and her sheep! They have won a Family Fun weekend at Sugarland Park Hotel!"

Angelica couldn't believe her ears.

"A *hotel*? What happened to yummy cookies and cake at Sugarland Park? Of all the crummy—"

But nobody heard Angelica. They were clapping too loudly.

"Bravo! Bravo!" yelled the crowd.

The babies laughed and took a bow.